UNDER MY HIJAB

by HENA KHAN

illustrated by AALIYA JALEEL

Lee & Low Books Inc. 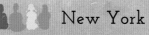 New York

Edited by Cheryl Klein • Book design by Kimi Weart • Book production by The Kids at Our House
The text is set in Josefin Slab • The illustrations are rendered in Adobe Photoshop

MIX
Paper from
responsible sources
FSC® C104723

Manufactured in China by Toppan
10 9 8 7 6 5 4 3 2 1
First Edition

Library of Congress Cataloging-in-Publication Data
Names: Khan, Hena, author. | Jaleel, Aaliya, illustrator.
Title: Under my hijab / by Hena Khan ; illustrated by Aaliya Jaleel. • Description: First edition. | New York, NY : Lee & Low Books, [2018] |
Summary: As a young girl observes that each of six women in her life wears her hijab and hair in a different way, she considers how to express her own style one day.
Identifiers: LCCN 2018025659 | ISBN 9781620147924 (hardback) • Subjects: | CYAC: Stories in rhyme. | Hijab (Islamic clothing)—Fiction. |
Clothing and dress—Fiction. | Individuality—Fiction. | Muslims—Fiction. | Classification: LCC PZ8.3.K493 Und 2018 | DDC [E]—dc23
LC record available at https://lccn.loc.gov/2018025659

To my strong Muslim sisters everywhere
—H.K.

To all the inspiring women in my life,
most importantly, my mom
—A.J.

Grandma peeks into the oven
as a brown loaf of bread starts to rise.
Her hijab is carefully folded,
like the crusts on my favorite pies.

When she's at home in her kitchen,
Grandma fixes her hair in a bun.
We mix up some chocolate cookies
and share a sweet treat when they're done.

Mama makes jokes with her patient as she peers in his ears and his throat. Her bright pink hijab looks so cheerful tucked into her tidy white coat.

At home, Mama lets her long hair down as she rolls up the sleeves on her shirt. We laugh while we plant pretty flowers and make a big mess with the dirt.

Auntie works hard in her studio.
She's always dressed funky and cool!
Her silky hijab towers up high,
pinned with a handmade jewel.

I help hang my very own painting
on the wall of her colorful home.
Auntie's hair is streaked pink and purple—
a fine work of art she can comb.

Jenna's our fearless troop leader.
She makes us the gooiest s'mores!
Her hijab is topped with a sun hat
whenever we hike the outdoors.

When dark falls, we huddle together
and share spooky stories all night.
Jenna's hair glows as she whispers.
I shiver and hold her arm tight.

My sister, Zayna, in high school, wears something stylish each day. She puts on a fashionable outfit and wraps her hijab a cute way.

Zayna ties up her hair in the evening
when she takes a short break from her book.
Then we dig through the clothes in her closet
to find her tomorrow's fresh look.

Iman tries to earn her first black belt.
A sporty hijab frames her face.
When she cracks a board into pieces,
I'm amazed her hijab stays in place.

At my house, we dance to some music.
I teach Iman moves that I know.
My cousin's curls bounce, jump, and tumble
as we put on our own private show.

These wonderful girls and smart women
inspire me with all that they do.
I can wear my hijab like each of them
or try something totally new.

Under my hijab, in a headband,
or a clip with butterfly wings,
my hair shines bright—like my future.
I can't wait to see what it brings.

ABOUT THE HIJAB

Like many other religions, Islam asks its followers, both men and women, to dress in a modest way. *Hijab* is a common word for the headscarf that millions of Muslim women wear to cover their hair and often their ears, necks, and chests. They may choose to dress in the hijab to reflect their faith, to feel closer to God, or because they believe their religion requires them to keep these parts of the body private.

Women put on the scarf when they go to work or school, play sports, or do any activity in a public setting. But they uncover when they are at home, with the men in their immediate families, or in the company of other women and girls. Young girls may practice wearing a hijab as part of a school uniform or to mirror the women in their lives. However, most girls don't wear the hijab regularly until adolescence.

It is important to note that many observant Muslim women, including the author of this book, choose not to wear a hijab, based on their personal interpretations of Islamic religious requirements. Yet they may cover their hair in certain situations, such as when visiting a mosque or while praying. As you saw on these pages, the hijab, like other types of clothing, is worn in many different styles depending on a person's individual taste and culture, and it can be a beautiful expression of the Islamic faith.